Big Little Brother

Thank you to Mary Ludington, Collette Morgan, Steven Kling, Dora Dysart Kling, Laura Wills, Mary McGeheran, Shannon Pennefeather, Ann Regan, Pam McClanahan, Dan Leary, and the amazing Chris Monroe.

—K K

With thanks to Dann Edholm, Mickey Sweere, Nancy Spellerberg, Meg Monroe, Paul Petersen, Alex Beyering, Scott Lunt, Barb Goranson, Britt Aamodt, Pam McClanahan, Super Dan Leary, and the incomparable Kevin Kling.

—C M

Storyteller Kevin Kling is the author of two books and several plays, including the musical *Busytown*, with composer Michael Koerner, based on the classic and amusing picture books by Richard Scarry.

Painter and cartoonist Chris Monroe draws the weekly comic strip *Violet Days* and is the author and illustrator of *Monkey with a Tool Belt* and *Sneaky Sheep*, among other books for children.

Borealis Books is an imprint of the Minnesota Historical Society Press.

www.mhspress.org

The Minnesota Historical Society Press is a member of the Association of American University Presses.

Book design by Anders Hanson, Mighty Media

Manufactured in Canada

10 9 8 7 6 5 4 3 2 1

∞ The paper used in this publication meets the minimum requirements of the American National Standard for Information Sciences— Permanence for Printed Library Materials, ANSI Z39.48-1984.

INTERNATIONAL STANDARD BOOK NUMBER
ISBN: 978-0-87351-844-4 (cloth)

LIBRARY OF CONGRESS CATALOGING-IN-PUBLICATION DATA
Kling, Kevin, 1957–
Big little brother / Kevin Kling ; illustrations by Chris Monroe.
p. cm.
Summary: A four-year-old boy explains that his little brother is bigger than he is, follows him everywhere, and is annoying, but his presence becomes indispensable when bullies are around.
ISBN 978-0-87351-844-4 (cloth : alk. paper)
[1. Brothers—Fiction. 2. Size—Fiction.] I. Monroe, Chris, ill. II. Title.
PZ7.K6797585Bi 2011
[E]—dc23
2011018586

BIG
LITTLE BROTHER

KEVIN
KLING

CHRIS
MONROE

DEDICATED TO
LITTLE BROTHERS

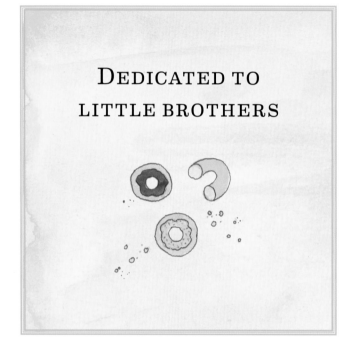

It's my own fault.

I wanted a little brother.

Then he grew … and GREW …
and kept growing until we were the same size.

3 months
↓

12 months
↓

16 months
↓

18 months
↓

me - 4 years
↓

But he kept growing.

Now people think he is my older brother.

I have a big-boy bed,

and he is in a crib.

I have pajamas,

and he's in a diaper.

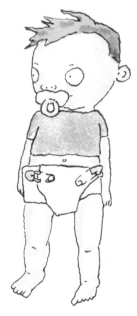

He loves to eat.

Especially donuts.

He grabs the first donut he sees and holds it all day.

We live on a busy road.

At night
when we
go to bed,
the headlights
of passing cars
make scary
shadows
across
our room.

He cries,
so Mom
sings to him:

Goodnight, brother
Goodnight, brother
Goodnight, brother . . .
We all love you so.

When he falls
asleep at night,

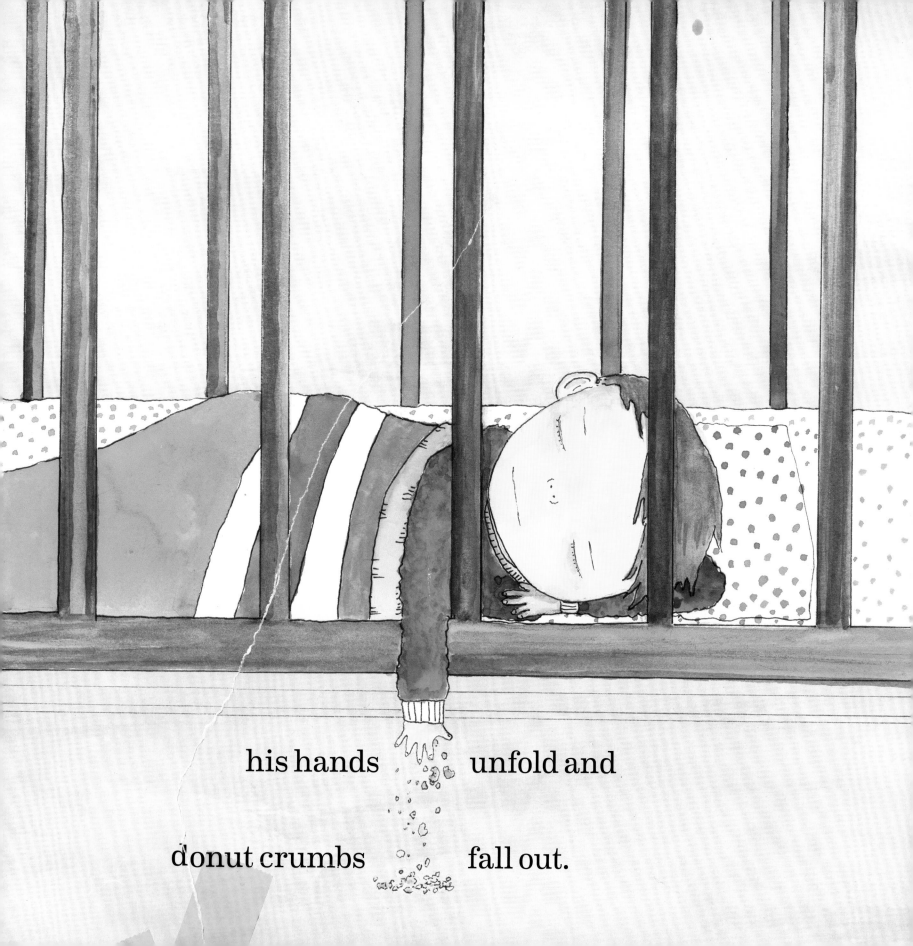

his hands   unfold and

donut crumbs   fall out.

In the morning, he goes
straight to touching all my toys.

And follows me everywhere.

Oh, he makes
me mad!

The only peace I have
is when Mom drops
me off at the Old
Woman in the Shoe,
a place for kids to stay
while moms shop.

Best of all, my brother
is too young to go there.

I've never seen the Old Woman, but her giant shoe is still there. It is full of toys, trucks and blocks, stuffed animals, and crayons and paper.

My favorite is the kitchen.

It has kid-sized stoves
and refrigerators and spoons.

I can make a whole Thanksgiving dinner by the time
Mom returns, but I have to get straight to work.

I put the tasty plastic turkey in the oven,

but another kid
walks up to the stove
and takes it out.

He just stands there holding the turkey, *my turkey*. I have an idea, but Mom says, "Remember to ask with our words, not with our teeth."

So I say:

That's mine.

And I take it back.

He pushes me down. *Hard.*

I want to cry, but I stand up.

The kid takes a step toward me.

"Uh-oh."

Then he stops.

That's when I see my big little
brother standing next to me.

With his largeness and
his fists full of donuts.

The
kid
walks
away.

Thanksgiving has been saved.

I cook the rest of the meal in peace.

Mom says from now on she'll leave
my brother with me while she shops.

He isn't much help in the kitchen,

but he is a good eater.

At home, he still touches my things...

and follows me.

Somehow it isn't so annoying.

At night when the headlights come,
I sing to him:

Goodnight, brother . . .

Goodnight, brother . . .

Goodnight,
brother . . .

We all love you so.

We all love you so.